The Kitten Psychologist Broaches The Topic of Economics

THEA VAN DIEPEN

OTHER WORKS

WHITE CHANGELING SERIES

Hidden In Sealskin
Like Mist Over The Eyes

THE UNDEAD FAIRY TALES COLLECTION

The Illuminated Heart

Dreaming Of Her And Other Stories
The Tree Remembers

Find other works by the author at
https://www.theavandiepen.com

The Kitten Psychologist Broaches The Topic of Economics

INKLETS #6

THEA VAN DIEPEN

Inkprint PRESS
www.inkprintpress.com

ISBN: 978-1-925825-06-0
eBook ISBN: 9781386782551

www.inkprintpress.com

*National Library of Australia Cataloguing-in-Publication
Data*
van Diepen, Thea
The Kitten Psychologist Broaches The Topic of
Economics
26 p.
ISBN: 978-1-925825-06-0
Inkprint Press, Canberra, Australia
1. Fiction—Animals 2. Fiction—Short Stories

First Print Edition: March 2019
Cover design © Inkprint Press
Interior art © Amy Laurens

THE KITTEN PSYCHOLOGIST BROACHES THE TOPIC OF ECONOMICS

THERE ONCE WAS A LITTLE KITTEN. NO, not the kitten I wrote a story about last time.

Definitely a different kitten. A very different kitten.

Oh, fine. It's the same kitten. So I'm reusing characters. So what?

This kitten had had a hard time going outside. Which is as much to say as it didn't. Not after its first experience with snow, which is probably like a person's first experience with horseradish: you either like it or you don't. And, in this case, the kitten didn't like it.

In the last story, wherein the kitten realized that there was probably maybe some benefit to going outside after paying me good money to sit around and ask it questions containing answers that it decided it had come up with all on its own, I wondered what I was doing with my life being a psychologist to my friends' nine week old kitten.

The only problem with this picture (I mean, aside from the obvious) was that the kitten wasn't paying me out of its own money. Let's be serious: I can be a kitten psychologist all I want, but we have to admit that a kitten having its own income stream at nine weeks stretches credibility quite thin.

Which is as much to say as that this kitten had mastered the use of arcane computer enchantments and pulled the money from my friends'—its owners'—bank account.

Frankly, I thought my friends would have figured it out on their own. It might have been a bit cowardly of me to wait until they got a clue and started investigating, but either this kitten was more clever than I thought or my friends had an awful memory for their own spending habits.

I'm not actually sure which was more concerning—but I had plenty of concern on hand to spend no matter which it turned out to be.

In other words, while my friends were out of the country a couple of weeks later, I house-sat. And, as I sat the house, I had a conversation with my friends' kitten.

"You really have to stop this," I said.

"I don't pay you to have an opinion," the kitten said with a swish of its tail.

"You pay me to be a psychologist.

That's exactly the same as paying me to have an opinion."

"What happened to unbiased objectivity?"

"Fine. In my unbiased, objective *opinion*, you have to stop this."

The kitten tapped its chin. "Stop what?"

"Paying me from my friends' bank account without their knowledge or consent." As if it didn't already know.

"If you don't like it, I can always find another psychologist..."

"That's not the point."

"And how do you propose I tell them about it when the idea of my sentience is patently absurd to them? Certainly *you* can't. They already think you're crazy."

Obviously, I was going to have to have a conversation with more than just the kitten. "And how would you inform a potential new psychologist of this patently absurd idea?"

"That's different. They're not my human. They aren't used to me. They don't have ingrained habits or ideas about me to contend with."

I bit back a sarcastic remark about the strength of eleven-week-old habits. For the kitten, that was a lifetime. That and it wasn't as if I hadn't had plenty of ingrained habits and ideas of my own about the nature of kittens when this one hired me.

I wondered if maybe I should have kept one or two of them. No amount of income was worth this trouble.

Well. Perhaps not certain amounts of income.

"Well, just give it some thought and see what happens," I finally said.

The kitten avoided me after that.

Which could have been the end of that, I suppose. Certainly it seemed like it, which I was a bit peeved about, to be sure. But, in a few days, I received an email:

Come at once. My humans are away. Sincerely, you know who.

I wondered if the kitten had finally got to my friends' YA collection. That and I went.

"So, I told my humans."

"How did they take it?"

"Now *they're* seeing a psychologist."

"Oh."

Silence.

"You know"—the kitten stretched—"I've come to a realization."

"Oh?"

"This is a ridiculous situation. I'm a kitten. Why do I even need a psychologist?"

I shrugged.

"Exactly. I should be going my wild way on my wild lone. Except..." It glanced at the couch. "...I don't think I'm prepared to give up the amenities of my current living situation."

"Then don't."

"Oh, I'm not. This may not be ancient Egypt, but it's certainly something. Do you suppose you could talk to my humans? Now that I have, that is."

And admit that I'd been complicit in what was essentially theft? Um. "No."

"Drat. I had a feeling this was my fight."

Sure. That's exactly what it was.

"Well, do you have any advice on what I should do next? Some words of wisdom I'll probably ignore when I inevitably come up with something better? Like nothing? I rather like the idea of doing nothing."

"If you'll just come up with something better, then why do you need my advice?"

No, theft was too harsh a word. Underhanded dealing, perhaps?

"It's amusing."

"So, am I psychologist or court jester?"

"Whichever makes you feel better, I suppose." The kitten yawned. "I'm going to have a nap. If you come up with something, email me. Or stop by. I'll pay you as soon as you do."

Who was I kidding? It was definitely theft. By the time I'd gotten home, I realized that. I also realized that, despite the fact that the kitten really should be acting responsibly with its humans, so should I with my friends. With a sigh, I picked up the phone.

I wondered how long I'd be paying them back.

Dear psychologist human,

I'm not entirely sure what you stood to gain by informing my humans of your part in all this. My intention had been for you to merely vouch for my sentience. You have done me a service, and it is right that you should be compensated in turn, not that you should throw that all away.

But no matter. We shall speak when you return from vacation. I think you will see things much more clearly when this is all over.

Sincerely,
You know who.

THE MAKING OF
THE KITTEN PSYCHOLOGIST BROACHES THE TOPIC OF ECONOMICS

Sometime after sending out *The Kitten Psychologist* to my email list, I came back to it, this time for my blog. And I wondered: how on *earth* was a kitten paying a psychologist?

Through immorality, of course.

At which point our psychologist, who couldn't *not* be aware of what was going on, had to grow a conscience and talk to the kitten about the situation.

To continue the tradition of kittens and psychologists being therapy for me, it turned out that, at the time, I was having issues standing up for myself and saying no to things that weren't good for me. At the same time, I was really unsure about managing money and how to do that effectively, and whether I'd ever make enough money to pay my bills, never mind everything else.

Which, obviously, meant it was time to convince a kitten to remember how to behave in a more... mature fashion. Yes. Let's put it that way.

DOWNLOAD YOUR FREE EBOOK

When you buy a print book from Inkprint Press, we like to say THANK YOU by offering you the ebook for free!

Please head to
www.inkprintpress.com/inklets/6/
and the use the coupon 6INKLET to get your copy of this Inklet in epub AND mobi today!
(Coupon will only work once.)

READ MORE!

DREAMING OF HER AND OTHER STORIES

A collection of short stories and poetry, written as refreshers, reminders of what makes life beautiful. Pieces include a story of the life of a river as he discovers his true self, a poetic retelling of Daphne's flight from Apollo, and, in the titular story, a literal nightmare as a girl comes to terms with the death of her sister.

https://www.theavandiepen.com

ABOUT THE AUTHOR

THEA VAN DIEPEN spent the first ten years of her life on a tree-wrapped acreage where an inquisitive child might believe in magic. Nowadays, she lives in Edmonton, breathing life into stories in the form of books such as the *White Changeling* series, a webcomic, and a video game.

Her website is theavandiepen.com, where she can be contacted in English and French... so long as you don't ask her to count in French, as she tends to miss numbers ending in six entirely by accident.

INKLETS

Collect them all! Released on the 1st and 15th of each month.

INKLET #007
SEVENTY
LIANA BROOKS

INKLET #008
A Final Request for Mercy
AMY LAURENS

INKLET #009
the kitten psychologist
vs.
the kitten's owners
THEA VAN DIEPEN

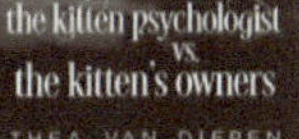

INKLET #010
Answer the Question
AMY LAURENS

INKLET #011
Happily, Red
AMY LAURENS

INKLET #012
the kitten psychologist
tries to be patient
through email
THEA VAN DIEPEN

INKLET #013
DRAGON Tuesday
AMY LAURENS

INKLET #014
RED PLANET REFUGEES
LIANA BROOKS

INKLET #015
the kitten psychologist &
What The Kitten Did
THEA VAN DIEPEN

INKLET #016
Cherry Blossom
AMY LAURENS

INKLET #017
Alone
AMY LAURENS

INKLET #018
the kitten psychologist & The Kitten Come To A Conclusion
THEA VAN DIEPEN

INKLET #019
LEVEL NINE
LIANA BROOKS

INKLET #020
To Dust
AMY LAURENS

INKLET #021
Interchange
AMY LAURENS

INKLET #022
Emalia's Lanterns
LIANA BROOKS

INKLET #023
Dear Santa
AMY LAURENS

INKLET #024
The Quilt-Maker's Scrap
AMY LAURENS